House of Incest

ANAÏS NIN

House of Incest

Foreword by Gunther Stuhlmann

Introduction by Allison Pease

SWALLOW PRESS • OHIO UNIVERSITY PRESS

ATHENS

Swallow Press
An imprint of Ohio University Press, Athens, Ohio 45701
© 1958 by Anaïs Nin
Foreword © 1994 by Gunther Stuhlmann
Introduction © 2020 by Allison Pease

First Swallow Press/Ohio University Press edition published 1979
To obtain permission to quote, reprint, or otherwise reproduce
or distribute material from Swallow Press / Ohio University Press
publications, please contact our rights and permissions department
at (740) 593-1154 or (740) 593-4536 (fax).

Printed in the United States of America
Swallow Press / Ohio University Press books are printed on acid-free
paper ⊗ ™

Library of Congress Control Number: 2019955314

ISBN (2020 paperback edition): 978-0-8040-1226-3

Library of Congress Cataloging-in-Publication Data
Nin, Anaïs, 1903-1977
    House of incest / Anaïs Nin:
    photomontages by Val Telberg.
    p. cm.
    ISBN 0-8040-0148-0
    1. Title
PS3527.I865H6 1989
811'.54—dc20   91-11993
                                       CIP

Contents

Foreword to the 1994 Edition

"I have written the first two pages of my new book in a surrealist way," Anaïs Nin noted in her *Diary* in April 1932. "I am influenced by *transition* and Breton and Rimbaud. They give my imagination an opportunity to leap freely." By July 1932, she had done "thirty pages of poetical prose, written in an absolutely imaginative manner, a lyrical outburst."

This creative "outburst" occurred at a time when Anaïs Nin's personal life was in great emotional turmoil. Determined to be recognized as a creative artist, she had been struggling for almost a decade with various eventually aborted novel projects while, at the same time, devoting herself untiringly to the keeping of her private diary. Her latest fiction project had been an attempt to come to grips with her disturbing infatuation with the writer John Erskine, her husband's friend and mentor, which had caused the first fissure in the fabric of her idealistic marriage to Hugh Guiler, the "banker-poet." A series of stories, expressing in still tentative glimpses a growing restlessness she openly confided now only to the secret pages of her diary, had made the rounds of American magazines and, unsurprisingly, had found no takers. (Published posthumously in the collection *Waste of Timelessness,* these early stories, in the guise of fiction, present some vivid images of Anaïs Nin's then state of mind and the concerns she explored more fully in her later work.) She had just finished, in record time, her *D. H. Lawrence: An Unprofessional Study,* her appreciation and defense of the just deceased, embattled writer—the first by a woman—which shocked some members of her Catholic family, and which, implicitly, raised the flag of her own sexual awakening. At the time, Anaïs Nin the woman was straining to break out of the confines of her sheltered life, her child-bride marriage, the stifling social atmosphere of her husband's business world, symbolized so perfectly by the creaky iron gate of their rented house in Louveciennes from where at times the luminous city of Paris could be glimpsed in the distance.

The catalyst of her breaking-out became the then unknown, middle-aged writer Henry Miller, the "gangster author," and his mythomaniacal wife, who occasionally turned up for a brief visit. June, the former New York taxi-dancer, seemed to Anaïs Nin to be the perfect incarnation of a female sexuality she herself had until then never dared to express or to explore except in her imagination. Her encounter with Miller and his wife turned into a central experience in her life

and her evolving love affair with Miller would domi-
nate her emotions for many years to come. The new
life Anaïs Nin now embraced, shedding all sexual inhi-
bitions within and outside of her marriage, became
increasingly complex and complicated. She found herself involved with the unstable actor-genius Antonin
Artaud, with her first analyst, Dr René Allendy, soon to
be followed by her second one, Dr Otto Rank, and sun-
dry other demanding and draining relationships. Trying to cope with these experiences in her writing she
found the perfect symbolization of the self-image that
seems to have possessed her at the time in the figure
of "Alraune," the woman "no man could satisfy," the
central character in a German film, based on a novel by
Hanns Heinz Ewers, which appeared in France under
the title *"La Mandragore."*

When she showed Henry Miller these first "surrealist" pages of the manuscript, which for a number of
years bore the working title "Alraune," he seemed mys-
tified. He asked her to explain her "abstractions" which,
of course, were the result of her effort to disguise the
true circumstances of her experiences. According to
her recollection, she told Miller: "I see the symbolism
in our lives. I live on two levels, the human and the
poetic. I see the parables, the allegories." In her per-
ception, Miller was "doing the realism" in probing the
perplexing, mysterious nature of WOMAN in the person of June, his second wife, the "Mara" and "Mona"
of his later work, while she—in the symbolic figure

of "Alraune" (later renamed "Sabina")—presented her own, multidimensional image of June as an extension, a missing aspect, a kind of *"Doppelgänger,"* of her own fragmented multiple selves. "I could go up in my stratosphere and survey the mythology of June," she wrote. "I sought to describe overtones. All the facts about June are useless in my visionary perceptions of her unconscious self. This was a distillation. But it was no mere brocade; it was full of meaning."

Anaïs Nin, in fact, persistently called this slim volume an attempt to come to grips, artistically, with her own personal "season in hell." It was a "corrosive" fiction, she thought, a poetic, lyrical transformation of experiences she had initially captured in all their emotional shadings in the still secret pages of her lifelong diary. It was material, she obviously felt, that needed to be revealed, confessed, but that could be presented—given the circumstances of her real life situation—only in the guise of a "fairy tale."

The published portions of Anaïs Nin's *Diary* of the early 1930s, in both the edited and the unexpurgated versions, provide indeed many clues to the characters, situations, and writing techniques employed in the evolving manuscript, which eventually appeared under the title *The House of Incest*. There are lengthy discussions recorded with Henry Miller about the uses of dreams in writing, the condensation and telescoping of images found, for instance, in some of the sequences in Luis Buñuel and Salvador Dali's film *Un chien Andalou,* that surrealist classic of 1928, where, in her words, "nothing is mentioned or verbalized." With Miller Anaïs Nin analyzes "the feeling one has in a dream of having made a long and wonderful speech, yet only a few phrases remain. It is like the state described by drug addicts. They imagine themselves utterly eloquent, and say very little. It is like the process of creation when, for a whole day, we carry in us a tumultuous sea of ideas, and when we reach home it can be stated in one page."

After reading Octave Mirbeau's notorious, post-de-Sadean classic *Le jardin du supplices* (1898), Anaïs Nin was inspired to try in her manuscript to produce "the counterpart of physical torture in the psychological," to convey "the very real suffering" of some of her friends, like June Miller, Antonin Artaud, or Louise de Vilmorin. "Physical tortures are banal and familiar," she noted, but "each one of these tortures, transposed onto a psychological plane, would make a novel." Thus, she set out in her writing to find the equivalent, the analogy for the physical in the psychological. "Take for instance the peeling of the skin," she wrote. "That could become the symbol of hypersensitiveness. The death by the loudness of the church bells would be the sound of hallucinations." Such symbolic transposition "became the theme of *House of Incest* and it helped to coordinate the description of anxieties."

Anaïs Nin also tried, for some time, to incorporate in her June/Alraune manuscript details of the emotionally shattering reunion with the father who had deserted the family some twenty years earlier, a loss that had so permanently affected her. But what she called the "human" story—revealed only recently in the diary volume *A Journal of Love: Incest*—resisted all "poetic" distillation. A more "realistic" version of the "Father story," purged of essential detail, eventually found its way into her second published work of fiction, *The Winter of Artifice* (1939). The choice of the title for the "Alraune" story, obviously, owes something to this wrenching experience, and speculation about the implications of *House of Incest* in later years indeed never quite abated.

Other "dreams and moods" from the original diary pages were absorbed and transposed into the text of "Alraune"—a practice underlying most of Anaïs Nin's later "fictions," which emerged from actual experiences recorded in her diary. It is not difficult, therefore, to trace the real persons and events on which the "surreal" montage disguises of Anaïs Nin's prose poem are based. Situated in a new and complex psychological reality, there is the figure of June/Alraune/Sabina, representing the multiple aspects of the author's own self-image; there, under the glass bell of social convention is "Jeanne," bound to her brothers in a "childhood marriage," clearly inspired by Louise de Vilmorin; there, at the Louvre, is Artaud in front of the symbolically significant painting of "Lot and His Daughter"; and there is Helba Huara, the Peruvian dancer, at the Théâtre in the Rue de la Gaieté, performing the dance of the woman without arms, a poignant finish to Anaïs Nin's poetic distillations.

In the fall of 1934, Anaïs Nin took the much revised manuscript with her to New York—but no publisher was interested. Henry Miller, still baffled but also intrigued enough to work with her on the manuscript, provided a "review" and a "preface"; Otto Rank, too, labored over an "introduction" which dealt with the figure of Alraune rather than Anaïs Nin's writing. (Never used, these texts appeared for the first time in the 1980s in *ANAIS: An International Journal*.) In the summer of 1935, plans finally materialized in Paris to bring out the new, retitled manuscript under the imprint of the "Siana" press (i.e. Anaïs spelled backward), the self-publishing venture of the "Villa Seurat" series, conceived in Henry Miller's studio at Number 18, which also served as Anaïs Nin's "office" away from her married life.

The first "huge bundles from the printer" arrived at her doorstep in Paris in May 1936, as she recorded in her *Diary*. There were altogether 249 copies of the 94-page book, printed at the Saint Catherine Press in Bruges, Belgium. They were numbered, and to be signed by the author.

When Henry Miller sent a copy of the book to his new-found friend Lawrence Durrell in Corfu, the young English writer wrote back that the book was "fresh and sweet and squeezes itself into sudden malleable shapes and colors." But it was Stuart Gilbert, the friend and translator of James Joyce into French, who provided in a few lines—in a preface never used—perhaps the most illuminating and still valid key to Anaïs Nin's lyrical outburst:

> The title of the book, *The House of Incest,* designates the exploration of an unknown world. According to her, in the world of passion each lover creates the being he loves, the loved one is a creation or a projection of the lover, a phantom born of his imagination; he loves something that is part of himself, he identifies with the loved one, and therefore this love of an unreal image is an act of incest. To my mind nothing like this has ever been written. To see love, one must be situated at the core of life itself, within ecstasy itself; one must be a poet.

At times, Anaïs Nin feared that she "had carried [her] fantasy so far that it was inexplicable to others." But by 1939 she was able to write: "I recognize the metaphysical authenticity. Writing like *House of Incest* and all the fantasies for which I will not be loved, contain the purest essence of my meaning." With her first published work of fiction Anaïs Nin had taken a stance against what she felt were the cold, reductive demands of mere analysis ("I think it is the poet in me affirming itself because of the struggle against psychoanalysis."). She had rebelled against the then prevailing "naturalists" and "reporters of facts," and even against the "realism" practiced by someone as close to her as Henry Miller. Courageously, she had followed what she called her own "law of writing," which held that it was essential to "formulate without destroying with the mind, without tampering, without killing, without withering." While in her later work Anaïs Nin never again employed the specific "surrealist" mode of *House of Incest*, this initial "lyrical outburst" had provided her with the courage and the means to use explosive, "death dealing" material from her secret diary, from the inner sanctum of her life, in the public arena of her art. "What is it allotted me to say?" she wrote in these pages. "Only the truth disguised in a fairy tale."

Becket, Massachusetts, Spring 1994
Gunther Stuhlmann

Introduction

ALLISON PEASE

Anaïs Nin was an extraordinary and daring writer whose life epitomized the upheavals, contradictions, and chaos of the twentieth century. In her quest for a unified self she embraced change and defied convention. Married at age twenty to a banker, she underwent psychoanalysis; engaged in sexual affairs with dozens of short- and long-term partners, including her father; shuttled between bigamous, bicoastal marriages, one in Los Angeles and one in New York; experimented with drugs; published her own work when no one else would; and eschewed feminism until she embraced it. She never gave up on her dream of becoming famous, a dream she did not realize until the final decade of her life, after the publication of her diaries. Anaïs Nin was a woman whose opportunities were forged by new realities for women in Europe and North America in the twentieth century, including, most importantly for her, artistic vocation and optional motherhood. As an artist and a woman coming of age after the first wave of feminism, Nin was able to cultivate her mind and her self. The mind's pursuit of selfhood and the self-in-others is the story around which *House of Incest* centers.

Born in 1903 in Neuilly-sur-Seine, a suburb of Paris, Anaïs Nin was the eldest of three children of a Cuban father, Joaquín Nin, and a Danish-French-Cuban mother, Rosa Culmell. The family moved frequently as Joaquín Nin pursued an international career as a concert pianist. He abandoned his wife and children permanently when Anaïs was ten years old. Anaïs moved at age eleven to New York City with her mother and two brothers. It was on the voyage to the New World that Anaïs began a practice she would continue throughout her entire life: writing in a diary. She wrote in French until age seventeen, and then she switched to English, her third language after French and Spanish. Nin was a shy, introspective teenager who spent more time writing in her diary than doing anything else. A voracious reader, she convinced her mother that she had enough discipline to complete her own education and quit high school in Queens, New York, at age sixteen.

At age seventeen Nin's diary records a split self: the public Miss Nin who performs household chores and can be seen greeting the local priest, and the "impossible" Linotte who "must be hidden, hidden."[1] This idea of a public and a private self occupies a central place in Nin's life. At age twenty Nin married Hugh Guiler, a banker with an interest in art and diaries, who largely indulged Nin for the rest of her life. Together they moved to Paris in 1924 for Guiler's career. Nin concentrated on her writing and conducted numerous flirtations up until 1932 when she began a ten-year-long affair with Henry Miller. This was Miller's most fertile writing period, in which he published *Tropic of Cancer* (1934) and *Tropic of Capricorn* (1938), works Nin midwived with her husband's money and her ideas, editorial suggestions, and housekeeping. During her affair with Miller, Nin was also writing and pursuing other sexual affairs. She was challenged by Miller and another of her lovers, psychoanalyst Otto Rank, to stop pouring her writing into her diary and instead to redirect that energy into writing a novel. From 1932 to 1935 she drafted and revised what eventually became *The House of Incest*.

Nin's life in the 1930s was complicated and very full. She entered psychoanalysis with two well-known analysts, René Allendy and Otto Rank, and had sexual relationships with both of them. Other affairs ensued while Nin was keeping house with her husband and living part-time with Henry Miller, notably with Surrealist Antonin Artaud, Peruvian Marxist Gonzalo Moré, Columbia University professors John Erskine and Edmund Wilson, and, when she was aged thirty, her own father. With Miller's encouragement and Guiler's money, Nin paid to have three works published in the 1930s, *D. H. Lawrence: An Unprofessional Study* (1932), *The House of Incest* (1936), and *The Winter of Artifice* (1939).

Nin and Guiler moved back to New York in December 1939, as World War II began to affect daily Paris life. Though Miller followed Nin to New York, their affair began to wane. Her equally long-term affair with Gonzalo Moré persevered a few years longer in New York, during which time he worked for Nin at her self-created Gemor Press in Greenwich Village. There she hand-printed her first critical success, the collection of stories *Under a Glass Bell* (1944). Shortly thereafter Nin struck up a friendship with Gore Vidal, who helped her gain her first major publisher, E. P. Dutton, for whom he worked as an editor. Dutton published *Ladders to Fire* (1946) but, because of its poor critical reception, refused her next manuscript. Nin took *The Four-Chambered Heart* (1950), a thinly veiled story of her long affair with Moré, to Duell, Sloan and Pearce for publication, and it was met with better, if still mixed, critical reviews.

By this time Anaïs Nin was living a geographically divided life. Having agreed to the proposition of one of her young lovers, the twenty-eight-year-old actor Rupert Pole, to drive from New York to Los Angeles with him in 1947, she entered a romantic relationship with him that would lead her to marry him in 1955 while still married to Hugh Guiler. Though the marriage to Pole was eventually annulled in 1966 in deference to her original marriage and Nin's concern for Guiler once his financial fortunes fell, Nin lived with Pole part-time for two decades and full-time in the final decade of her life—ironically, after their marriage was annulled.

Despite rejections from at least eleven publishers, Nin published *A Spy in the House of Love* in 1954 through the British Book Centre thanks to Guiler's financial assistance, and then established the Anaïs Nin Press to sell copies of some of her out-of-print books as well as *Solar Barque* (1958). Her rough relationship with commercial publication was finally resolved when she approached Alan Swallow of Swallow Press in 1961 and he enthusiastically agreed to publish five of her works—*Seduction of the Minotaur* (a revision of *Solar Barque*), *House of Incest*, *Winter of Artifice*, *Under a Glass Bell*, and *Cities of the Interior*—under one title, *Cities of the Interior* (1961). In 1966 Nin began to realize the fame she had craved her entire life. Harcourt Brace published Volume 1 of her *Diary,* tracking the years 1931–34. Letters and reviews poured in, and she became a feminist icon whose talks were requested in the United States and Europe. Anaïs Nin died of cancer in California in January 1977 while her work was still being published and her fame was at its peak.

HOUSE OF INCEST

House of Incest is divided into seven sections, each marking passage from birth to freedom through forms of love that Nin saw, in their narcissism, as incestuous. To say this much is to attribute clarity and narrative form to what is generally without those things. Nin's method in the text has been called Surrealist or Symbolist, and in its untraditional form, registry of sensations and the inner life, personalized metaphors and imagery, privileging of dream, use of juxtaposition, and jarring unrealistic images, it partakes of both traditions.

One of Nin's lovers in the 1930s was Columbia University professor Edmund Wilson, author of the 1931 study *Axel's Castle*, which traced Symbolist literature from 1870 to 1930. Wilson's explanation of Symbolism in the book sheds light on some of the techniques Nin used to transform ideas and passages from her diaries into the form of *House of Incest*:

> Each poet has his unique personality; each of his moments has its special tone, its special combination of elements. And it is the poet's task to find, to invent, the special language which will alone be capable of expressing his personality and feelings. Such a language must make use of symbols: what is so special, so fleeting and so vague cannot be conveyed by direct statement or description, but only by a succession of words, of images, which will serve to suggest it to the reader. The Symbolists themselves, full of the idea of producing with poetry effects like those of music, tended to think of these images as possessing an abstract value like musical notes and chords. But the words of our speech are not musical notation, and what the symbols of Symbolism really

were, were metaphors detached from their subjects—for one cannot, beyond a certain point, in poetry, merely enjoy color and sound for their own sake: one has to guess what the images are being applied to. And Symbolism may be defined as an attempt by carefully studied means—a complicated association of ideas represented by a medley of metaphors—to communicate unique personal feelings.[2]

Wilson's book surveyed the writers W. B. Yeats, Paul Valéry, T. S. Eliot, Marcel Proust, James Joyce, Gertrude Stein, and Arthur Rimbaud. If one encounters difficulty in understanding Nin's *House of Incest*, it may be no more so than, and in a similar vein to, the texts of these writers. Eliot and Joyce, in the *Waste Land* and *Ulysses*, for instance, tied the narrative arcs of their works to western myths. *House of Incest*, in similar fashion, invokes "the modern Christ" as trying to lead those who love only themselves in the other from the sterile entrapment of time and place, the actual "house" of incest in which the narrator and the character Jeanne find themselves, to the outside world and "daylight."

House of Incest begins with a passage on the trauma of birth, a passage that may have been inspired by one of Nin's analysts and lovers, Otto Rank, whose 1924 book *The Trauma of Birth* was influential in its time. Images in section I denote water, limitation, and loss. The narrator conveys that she is "stuck" in water that is "veiled" and forms a "curtain." She experiences the primary loss, that of the infant in union with its mother-womb, in which one feels "loving without knowingness, moving without effort." This state is likened to a dream from which one rudely awakens.

In section 2 the narrator describes her love for Sabina, a goddess figure modeled after June Miller, who first captured Nin's interest when they met in 1932. This section emphasizes female knowledge of the self through the female other. They share mirror-like gazes—"Deep into each other we turned our harlot eyes"; and recognize one in the other—"I see in you that part of me which is you"; and eventually merge identities—"I become you. And you become me." The sexual embrace of these two women is the attempt to become the other and in doing so love the self. But it is a form of entrapment that does not sustain. The passage is full of images of enclosure and death, images that the narrator says bring a "dissolution of the soul within the body."

Throughout the text there is a struggle between reality and fantasy, Nin almost always preferring the dream but knowing that as much as it enlarges reality it also makes it false. In section 3 this struggle is foregrounded. The narrator finds herself trapped, in fact, by dreams: "The dream rings through me like a giant copper bell when I wish to betray it. It brushes by me with bat wings when I open human eyes and seek to live dreamlessly." The "Collison with reality blurs my vision and submerges me into the dream." In the final part of section 3 dreams are likened to the narrator's lies. She confesses that she lies because "the truth would be death-dealing and I prefer fairytales."

In sections 4–6 the narrative switches to third person and describes "Jeanne"— an alter-ego for the narrator—who has an incestuous relationship with her brother. This section has frequently been explained as Nin's description of her incestuous relationship with her father, most explicitly referenced in the painting the narrator finds of Lot with his hand on his daughter's breast. Jeanne is an artist, a musician, and behind her art is "her thirst, her hunger and her fears." Jeanne feels entrapped by everyday reality that intrudes on her fantasies. Yet those fantasies and the intensity with which she experiences them exact their own cost, the feverishness of living in extremis. This intensity results in a feeling of isolation and loneliness that both seeks one like oneself with whom to identify, and fears such an identification that would break through the isolation and remove one from the control of one's fantasy life.

The narrator speaks directly to Jeanne in section 4 to warn that "Worlds self-made and self-nourished are so full of ghosts and monsters." The narcissistic and incestuous love of Jeanne and her brother is "like one long shadow kissing, without hope of reality."

Section 5 describes the house of incest itself in which "everything had been made to stand still, and everything was rotting away." Time does not pass, nothing grows, and the narrator encounters a dreamscape of trees that fail to transmutate and eggs that show the "moist beginning worshipped rather than its flowering." The landscape, like that in T. S. Eliot's *The Waste Land,* is a negative scape, defined by that which it is not rather than that which it is.

In section 6 Jeanne goes hunting for a lost room in the house of incest where she hopes to find her brother. She finds him asleep among paintings where he tells her "I fell in love with your portrait, Jeanne, because it will never change." The link between incest, love of self and love of self in the other, as fear of growth and change is made complete here.

The final section of House of Incest, section 7, takes the biblical number seven of creation as its inspiration in order to see a created world in which "the modern Christ" leads the way to a different world. In this section the narrative is taken up by a first-person speaker relaying the journey of the book itself. She begins with a single line: "I walked into my own book, seeking peace." If the journey has been to seek peace, the way has been to move past the narcissistic and incestuous, dream of love that that is a by-product of the trauma of birth and to enter into reality. This is because, the narrator declares, "LIES CREATE SOLITUDE."

The modern Christ, all-seeing and all-feeling, seeks to save Sabina, Jeanne, and the narrator—all women— from the house of incest where they only love themselves in the other. But the women cannot bear to pass through the tunnel into the "the world on the other side of the walls, where there were leaves on the trees, where water ran beside the paths, where there was daylight and joy." Instead they can only look at a dancer "dancing the dance of the woman without arms" whose dancing "was isolated and separated from music and from us and from the room and from life." She is not a sign of promise but of warning. Her arms were taken from her as punishment for clinging and clutching "at the lovely moments of life." If all, including the self, is ephemeral, one must give and relinquish, like the dancer who, in the final passages, is seen "permitting all things to flow away and beyond her." The final image of *House of Incest* is of this dancer dancing to the "rhythm of earth's circles," and thus accepting time and one's flow within it as she dances "towards daylight." There is hope for those who accept time, the otherness of the self in time, and the otherness that is reality.

NOTES

1. *The Early Diary of Anaïs Nin, Vol. 1: 1914–1920 ("Linotte")*, trans. Jean L. Sherman (New York: Harcourt Brace Jovanovich, 1985), 30.

2. Edmund Wilson, *Axel's Castle: A Study of the Imaginative Literature of 1870–1930* (New York: Charles Scribner's Sons, 1931), 21–22.

House of Incest

All that I know is contained in this book
written without witness,
an edifice without dimension,
a city hanging in the sky.

The morning I got up to begin this book I coughed. Something was coming out of my throat: it was strangling me. I broke the thread which held it and yanked it out. I went back to bed and said: I have just spat out my heart.

There is an instrument called the quena made of human bones. It owes its origin to the worship of an Indian for his mistress. When she died he made a flute out of her bones. The quena has a more penetrating, more haunting sound than the ordinary flute.

Those who write know the process. I thought of it as I was spitting out my heart.

Only I do not wait for my love to die.

MY FIRST VISION OF EARTH WAS water veiled. I am of the race of men and women who see all things through this curtain of sea, and my eyes are the color of water.

I looked with chameleon eyes upon the changing face of the world, looked with anonymous vision upon my uncompleted self.

I remember my first birth in water. All round me a sulphurous transparency and my bones move as if made of rubber. I sway and float, stand on boneless toes listening for distant sounds, sounds beyond the reach of human ears, see things beyond the reach of human eyes. Born full of memories of the bells of the Atlantide. Always listening for lost sounds and searching for lost colors, standing forever on the threshold like one troubled with memories, and walking with a swimming stride. I cut the air with wide-slicing fins, and swim through wall-less rooms. Ejected from a paradise of soundlessness, cathedrals wavering at the passage of a body, like soundless music.

This Atlantide could be found again only at night, by the route of the dream. As soon as sleep covered the rigid new city, the rigidity of the new world, the heaviest portals slid open on smooth-oiled gongs and one entered the voicelessness of the dream. The terror and joy of murders accomplished in silence, in the silence of slidings and brushings. The blanket of water lying over all things stifling the voice. Only a monster brought me up on the surface by accident.

Lost in the colors of the Atlantide, the colors running into one another without frontiers. Fishes made of velvet, of organdie with lace fangs, made of spangled taffeta, of silks and feathers and whiskers, with lacquered flanks and rock crystal eyes, fishes of withered leather with gooseberry eyes, eyes like the white of egg. Flowers palpitating on stalks like sea-hearts. None of them feeling their own weight, the sea-horse moving like a feather . . .

It was like yawning. I loved the ease and the blindness and the suave voyages on the water bearing one through obstacles. The water was there to bear one like a giant bosom; there was always the water to rest on, and the water transmitted the lives and the loves, the words and the thoughts.

Far beneath the level of storms I slept. I moved within color and music as inside a sea-diamond. There were no currents of thoughts, only the caress of flow and desire mingling, touching, travelling, withdrawing, wandering— the endless bottoms of peace.

I do not remember being cold there, nor warm. No pain of cold and heat. The temperature of sleep, feverless and chilless. I do not remember being hungry. Food seeped through invisible pores. I do not remember weeping.

I felt only the caress of moving—moving into the body of another—absorbed and lost within the flesh of another, lulled by the rhythm of water, the slow palpitation of the senses, the movement of silk.

Loving without knowingness, moving without effort, in the soft current of water and desire, breathing in an ecstasy of dissolution.

I awoke at dawn, thrown up on a rock, the skeleton of a ship choked in its own sails.

THE NIGHT SURROUNDED ME, A
photograph unglued from its frame. The
lining of a coat ripped open like the two shells of
an oyster. The day and night unglued, and I falling
in between not knowing on which layer I was
resting, whether it was the cold grey upper leaf of
dawn, or the dark layer of night.

Sabina's face was suspended in the darkness of
the garden. From the eyes a simoun wind shrivelled
the leaves and turned the earth over; all things which
had run a vertical course now turned in circles,
round the face, around HER face. She stared with
such an ancient stare, heavy luxuriant centuries
flickering in deep processions. From her nacreous
skin perfumes spiralled like incense. Every gesture
she made quickened the rhythm of the blood and
aroused a beat chant like the beat of the heart of
the desert, a chant which was the sound of her feet
treading down into the blood the imprint of her face.

A voice that had traversed the centuries, so
heavy it broke what it touched, so heavy I feared it

would ring in me with eternal resonance; a voice rusty with the sound of curses and the hoarse cries that issue from the delta in the last paroxysm of orgasm.

Her black cape hung like black hair from her shoulders, half-draped, half-floating around her body. The web of her dress moving always a moment before she moved, as if aware of her impulses, and stirring long after she was still, like waves ebbing back to the sea. Her sleeves dropped like a sigh and the hem of her dress danced around her feet.

The steel necklace on her throat flashed like summer lightning and the sound of the steel was like the clashing of swords . . . *Le pas d'acier* . . . The steel of New York's skeleton buried in granite, buried standing up. *Le pas d'acier* . . . notes hammered on the steel-stringed guitars of the gypsies, on the steel arms of chairs dulled with her breath; steel mail curtains falling like the flail of hail, steel bars and steel barrage cracking. Her necklace thrown around the world's neck, unmeltable. She carried it like a trophy wrung of groaning machinery, to match the inhuman rhythm of her march.

The leaf fall of her words, the stained glass hues of her moods, the rust in her voice, the

smoke in her mouth, her breath on my vision like
human breath blinding a mirror.

Talk—half-talk, phrases that had no need to
be finished, abstractions, Chinese bells played on
with cotton-tipped sticks, mock orange blossoms
painted on porcelain. The muffled, close, half-talk
of soft-fleshed women. The men she had embraced, and the women, all washing against the
resonance of my memory. Sound within sound,
scene within scene, woman within woman—like
acid revealing an invisible script. One woman
within another eternally, in a far-reaching pro-
cession, shattering my mind into fragments, into
quarter tones which no orchestral baton can ever
make whole again.

The luminous mask of her face, waxy, immobile, with eyes like sentinels. Watching my sybaritic
walk, and I the sibilance of her tongue. Deep into
each other we turned our harlot eyes. She was an
idol in Byzance, an idol dancing with legs parted;
and I wrote with pollen and honey. The soft secret
yielding of woman I carved into men's brains
with copper words; her image I tattooed in their
eyes. They were consumed by the fever of their
entrails, the indissoluble poison of legends. If the
torrent failed to engulf them, or they did extricate
themselves, I haunted their memory with the tale

they wished to forget. All that was swift and ma-
levolent in woman might be ruthlessly destroyed,
but who would destroy the illusion on which I
laid her to sleep each night? We lived in Byzance.
Sabina and I, until our hearts bled from the pre-
cious stones on our foreheads, our bodies tired of
the weight of brocades, our nostrils burned with
the smoke of perfumes; and when we had passed
into other centuries they enclosed us in copper
frames. Men recognized her always: the same
effulgent face, the same rust voice. And she and I,
we recognized each other; I her face and she my
legend.

Around my pulse she put a flat steel bracelet
and my pulse beat as she willed, losing its human
cadence, thumping like a savage in orgiastic frenzy.
The lamentations of flutes, the double chant of
wind through our slender bones, the cracking of
our bones distantly remembered when on beds of
down the worship we inspired turned to lust.

As we walked along, rockets burst from the
street lamps; we swallowed the asphalt road with
a jungle roar and the houses with their closed eyes
and geranium eyelashes; swallowed the telegraph poles trembling with messages; swallowed
stray cats, trees, hills, hedges, Sabina's labyrin-
thian smile on the keyhole. The door moaning,

opening. Her smile closed. A nightingale disleaf-
ing melliferous honeysuckle. Honey-suckled.
Fluted fingers. The house opened its green gate
mouth and swallowed us. The bed was floating.

The record was scratched, the crooning
broken. The pieces cut our feet. It was dawn and
she was lost. I put back the houses on the road,
aligned the telegraph poles along the river and
the stray cats jumping across the road. I put back
the hills. The road came out of my mouth like a
velvet ribbon—it lay there serpentine. The houses
opened their eyes. The keyhole had an ironic
curve, like a question mark. The woman's mouth.

I was carrying her fetiches, her marionettes,
her fortune teller's cards worn at the corners like
the edge of a wave. The windows of the city were
stained and splintered with rainlight and the blood
she drew from me with each lie, each deception.
Beneath the skin of her cheeks I saw ashes: would
she die before we had joined in perfidious union?
The eyes, the hands, the sense that only women
have.

There is no mockery between women. One
lies down at peace as on one's own breast.

Sabina was no longer embracing men and
women. Within the fever of her restlessness the
world was losing its human shape. She was losing

the human power to fit body to body in human completeness. She was delimiting the horizons, sinking into planets without axis, losing her polarity and the divine knowledge of integration, of fusion. She was spreading herself like the night over the universe and found no god to lie with. The other half belonged to the sun, and she was at war with the sun and light. She would tolerate no bars of light on open books, no orchestration of ideas knitted by a single theme; she would not be covered by the sun, and half the universe belonged to him; she was turning her serpent back to that alone which might overshadow her own stature giving her the joy of fecundation.

Come away with me, Sabina, come to my island. Come to my island of red peppers sizzling over slow *braseros,* Moorish earthen jars catching the gold water, palm trees, wild cats fighting, at dawn a donkey sobbing, feet on coral reefs and sea-anemones, the body covered with long sea-weeds, Melisande's hair hanging over the balcony at the Opéra Comique, inexorable diamond sunlight, heavy nerveless hours in the violaceous shadows, ash-colored rocks and olive trees, lemon trees with lemons hung like lanterns at a garden party, bamboo shoots forever trembling, soft-sounding espadrilles, pomegranates spurting blood, a flute-like Moorish chant, long and insistent, of the ploughmen, trilling, swearing, trilling and cursing, dropping perspiration on the earth with the seeds.

Your beauty drowns me, drowns the core of me. When your beauty burns me I dissolve as I never dissolved before man. From all men I was different, and myself, but I see in you that part of me which is you. I feel you in me; I feel my own voice becoming heavier, as if I were drinking you in, every delicate thread of resemblance being soldered by fire and one no longer detects the fissure.

Your lies are not lies, Sabina. They are arrows flung out of your orbit by the strength of your fantasy. To nourish illusion. To destroy reality. I will help you: it is I who will invent lies for you and with them we will traverse the world. But behind our lies I am dropping Ariadne's golden thread—to retrace one's lies, to return to the source and sleep one night a year washed of all superstructures.

Sabina, you made your impression upon the world. I passed through it like a ghost. Does anyone notice the owl in the tree at night, the bat which strikes the window pane while others are talking, the eyes which reflect like water and drink like blotting paper, the pity which flickers quietly

like candlelight, the understanding on which
people lay themselves to sleep?

DOES ANYONE KNOW WHO I AM?

Even my voice came from other worlds. I was
embalmed in my own secret vertigoes. I was suspended over the world, seeing what road I could
tread without treading down even clay or grass.
My step was a sentient step; the mere crepitation
of gravel could arrest my walk.

When I saw you, Sabina, I chose my body.

I will let you carry me into the fecundity of
destruction. I choose a body then, a face, a voice.
I become you. And you become me. Silence the
sensational course of your body and you will see in
me, intact, your own fears, your own pities. You will
see love which was excluded from the passions given
you, and I will see the passions excluded from love.
Step out of your role and rest yourself on the core of
your true desires. Cease for a moment your violent
deviations. Relinquish the furious indomitable strain.

I will take them up.

Cease trembling and shaking and gasping
and cursing and find again your core which I am.
Rest from twistedness, distortion, deformations.
For an hour you will be me; that is, the other half
of yourself. The half you lost. What you burnt,

broke, and tore is still in my hands: I am the keeper of fragile things and I have kept of you what is indissoluble.

Even the world and the sun cannot show their two faces at once.

So now we are inextricably woven. I have gathered together all the fragments. I return them to you. You have run with the wind, scattering and dissolving. I have run behind you, like your own shadow, gathering what you have sown in deep coffers.

I AM THE OTHER FACE OF YOU

Our faces are soldered together by soft hair, soldered together, showing two profiles of the same soul. Even when I passed through a room like a breath, I made others uneasy and they knew I had passed.

I was the white flame of your breath, your simoun breath shrivelling the world. I borrowed your visibility and it was through you I made my imprint on the world. I praised my own flame in you.

THIS IS THE BOOK YOU WROTE

AND YOU ARE THE WOMAN

I AM

Only our faces must shine twofold—like day and night—always separated by space and the evolutions of time.

The smoke sent my head to the ceiling: there it hung, looking down upon frog eyes, straw hair, mouth of soiled leather, mirrors of bald heads, furred monkey hands with ham-colored palms. The music whipped the past out of its tomb and mummies flagellated my memory.

If Sabina were now a memory; if I should sit here and she should never come again! If I only imagined her one night because the drug made fine incisions and arranged the layers of my body on Persian silk hammocks, tipped with cotton each fine nerve and sent the radium arrows of fantasy through the flesh . . .

I am freezing and my head falls down through a thin film of smoke. I am searching for Sabina again with deep anguish through the faceless crowd.

I am ill with the obstinacy of images, reflections in cracked mirrors. I am a woman with Siamese cat eyes smiling always behind my gravest words, mocking my own intensity. I smile because I listen to the OTHER and I believe the OTHER. I am a marionette pulled by unskilled fingers, pulled apart, inharmoniously dislocated; one arm

dead, the other rhapsodizing in mid-air. I laugh,
not when it fits into my talk, but when it fits into
the undercurrents of my talk. I want to know
what is running underneath thus punctuated by
bitter upheavals. The two currents do not meet. I
see two women in me freakishly bound together,
like circus twins. I see them tearing away from
each other. I can hear the tearing, the anger and
love, passion and pity. When the act of dislocation
suddenly ceases—or when I cease to be aware of
the sound—then the silence is more terrible because there is nothing but insanity around me, the
insanity of things pulling, pulling within oneself,
the roots tearing at each other to grow separately,
the strain made to achieve unity.

It requires only a bar of music to still the dislocation for a moment; but there comes the smile
again, and I know that the two of us have leaped
beyond cohesion.

Greyness is no ordinary greyness, but a vast
lead roof which covers the world like the lid of a
soup pan. The breath of human beings is like the
steam of a laundry house. The smoke of ciga-
rettes is like a rain of ashes from Vesuvius. The
lights taste of sulphur, and each face stares at you
with the immensity of its defects. The smallness
of a room is like that of an iron cage in which

one can neither sit nor lie down. The largeness
of other rooms is like a mortal anger always
suspended above you, awaiting the moment of
your joy to fall. Laughter and tears are not separate experiences, with intervals of rest: they rush
out together and it is like walking with a sword
between your legs. Rain does not wet your hair
but drips in the cells of the brain with the obstinacy of a leak. Snow does not freeze the hands,
but like ether distends the lungs until they burst.
All the ships are sinking with fire in their bowels,
and there are fires hissing in the cellars of every
house. The loved one's whitest flesh is what the
broken glass will cut and the wheel crush. The
long howls in the night are howls of death. Night
is the collaborator of torturers. Day is the light on
harrowing discoveries. If a dog barks it is the man
who loves wide gashes leaping in through the
window. Laughter precedes hysteria. I am waiting
for the heavy fall and the foam at the mouth.

A room with a ceiling threatening me like a
pair of open scissors. Attic windows. I lie on a bed
like gravel. All connections are breaking. Slowly
I part from each being I love, slowly, carefully,
completely. I tell them what I owe them and
what they owe me. I cull their last glances and
the last orgasm. My house is empty, sun-glazed,

reflectively alive, its stillness gathering implications, secret images which some day will madden
me when I stand before blank walls, hearing
far too much and seeing more than is humanly
bearable. I part from them all. I die in a small
scissor-arched room, dispossessed of my loves and
my belongings, not even registered in the hotel
book. At the same time I know that if I stayed in
this room a few days an entirely new life could
begin—like the soldering of human flesh after an
operation. It is the terror of this new life, more
than the terror of dying, which arouses me. I
jump out of bed and run out of this room growing around me like a poisoned web, seizing my
imagination, gnawing into my memory so that in
seven moments I will forget who I am and whom
I have loved.

It was room number 35 in which I might have
awakened next morning mad or a whore.

Desire which had stretched the nerve broke,
and each nerve seemed to break separately, continuously, making incisions, and acid ran instead
of blood. I writhed within my own life, seeking
a free avenue to carry the molten cries, to melt
the pain into a cauldron of words for everyone
to dip into, everyone who sought words for their
own pain. What an enormous cauldron I stir now;

enormous mouthfuls of acid I feed the others now, words bitter enough to burn all bitterness.

Disrupt the brown crust of the earth and all the sea will rise; the sea-anemones will float over my bed, and the dead ships will end their voyages in my garden. Exorcise the demons who ring the hours over my head at night when all counting should be suspended; they ring because they know that in my dreams I am cheating them of centuries. It must be counted like an hour against me.

I heard the lutes which were brought from Arabia and felt in my breasts the currents of liquid fire which run through the rooms of the Alhambra and refresh me from the too clear waters.

The too clear pain of love divided, love divided . . .

I was in a ship of sapphire sailing on seas of coral. And standing at the prow singing. My singing swelled the sails and ripped them; where they had been ripped the edge was burnt and the clouds too were ripped to tatters by my voice.

I saw a city where each house stood on a rock between black seas full of purple serpents hissing alarms, licking the rocks and peering over the walls of their gardens with bulbous eyes.

I saw the glass palm tree sway before my eyes; the palm trees on my island were still and dusty when I saw them deadened by pain. Green leaves withered for me, and all the trees seemed glassily unresponsive while the glass palm tree threw off a new leaf on the very tip and climax of its head.

The white path sprouted from the heart of the white house and was edged with bristly cactus long-fingered and furry, unmoved by the wind, ageless. Over the ageless cactus the bamboo shoots trembled, close together, perpetually wind-shirred.

The house had the shape of an egg, and it was carpeted with cotton and windowless; one slept in the down and heard through the shell the street organ and the apple vendor who could not find the bell.

Images—bringing a dissolution of the soul within the body like the rupture of sweet-acid of the orgasm. Images made the blood run back and forth, and the watchfulness of the mind watching against dangerous ecstasies was now useless. Reality was drowned and fantasies choked each hour of the day.

Nothing seems true today except the death of the goldfish who used to make love at ninety kilometers an hour in the pool. The maid has given him a Christian burial. To the worms! To the worms!

AM FLOATING AGAIN. ALL THE FACTS
and all the words, all images, all presages are
sweeping over me, mocking each other. The
dream! The dream! The dream rings through
me like a giant copper bell when I wish to betray
it. It brushes by me with bat wings when I open
human eyes and seek to live dreamlessly. When
human pain has struck me fiercely, when anger
has corroded me, I rise, I always rise after the
crucifixion, and I am in terror of my ascensions.
THE FISSURE IN REALITY. The divine departure. I fall. I fall into darkness after the collision
with pain, and after pain the divine departure.

Oh, the weight, the tremendous weight of
my head pulled up by the clouds and swing-
ing in space, the body like a wisp of straw, the
clouds dragging my hair like a scarf caught in a
chariot wheel, the body dangling, colliding with
the lantern stars, the clouds dragging me over
the world.

I cannot stop, or descend.

I hear the unfurling of water, of skies and curtains. I hear the shiver of leaves, the breathing of the air, the wailing of the unborn, the pressure of the wind.

I hear the movements of the stars and planets, the slight rust creak when they shift their position. The silken passage of radiations, the breath of circles turning.

I hear the passing of mysteries and the breathing of monsters. Overtones only, or undertones. Collision with reality blurs my vision and submerges me into the dream. I feel the distance like a wound. It unrolls itself before me like the rug before the steps of a cathedral for a wedding or a burial. It is unrolled like a crimson bride between the others and me, but I cannot walk on it without a feeling of uneasiness, as one has at ceremonies. The ceremony of walking along the unrolled carpet into the cathedral where the functions unravel to which I am a stranger. I neither marry or die. And the distance between the crowd, between the others and me, grows wider.

Distance. I never walked over the carpet into the ceremonies. Into the fullness of the crowd life, into the authentic music and the odor of men. I never attended the wedding or the burial. Everything for me took place either in the belfry where

I was alone with the deafening sound of bells calling in iron voices, or in the cellar where I nibbled at the candles and the incense stored away with the mice.

I cannot be certain of any event or place, only of my solitude. Tell me what the stars are saying about me. Does Saturn have eyes made of onions which weep all the time? Has Mercury chicken feathers on his heels, and does Mars wear a gas mask? Gemini, the evolved twins, do they evolve all the time, turning on a spit, Gemini *à la broche?*

There is a fissure in my vision and madness will always rush through. Lean over me, at the bedside of my madness, and let me stand without crutches.

I am an insane woman for whom houses wink and open their bellies. Significance stares at me from everywhere, like a gigantic underlying ghostliness. Significance emerges out of dank alleys and sombre faces, leans out of the windows of strange houses. I am constantly reconstructing a pattern of something forever lost and which I cannot forget. I catch the odors of the past on street corners and I am aware of the men who will be born tomorrow. Behind windows there are either enemies or worshippers. Never neutrality or passivity. Always intention and premeditation. Even stones have for me druidical expressions.

I walk ahead of myself in perpetual expectancy of miracles.

I am enmeshed in my lies, and I want absolution. I cannot tell the truth because I have felt the heads of men in my womb. The truth would be death-dealing and I prefer fairytales. I am wrapped in lies which do not penetrate my soul. As if the lies I tell were like costumes. The shell of mystery can break and grow again over night. But the moment I step into the cavern of my lies I drop into darkness. I see a face which stares at me like the glance of a cross-eyed man.

I remember the cold on Jupiter freezing ammonia and out of ammonia crystals came the angels. Bands of ammonia and methane encircling Uranus. I remember the tornadoes of inflammable methane on Saturn. I remember on Mars a vegetation like the tussock grasses of Peru and Patagonia, an ochrous red, a rusty ore vegetation, mosses and lichens. Iron bearing red clays and red sandstone. Light there had a sound and sunlight was an orchestra.

DILATED EYES NOBLE-RACED PROFILE, wilful mouth. Jeanne, all in fur, with fur eyelashes, walking with head carried high, nose to the wind, eyes on the stars, walking imperiously, dragging her crippled leg. Her eyes higher than the human level, her leg limping behind the tall body, inert, like the chained ball of a prisoner.

Prisoner on earth, against her will to die.

Her leg dragging so that she might remain on earth, a heavy dead leg which she carried like the ball and chain of a prisoner.

Her pale, nerve-stained fingers tortured the guitar, tormenting and twisting the strings with her timidity as her low voice sang; and behind her song, her thirst, her hunger and her fears. As she turned the keys of her guitar, fiercely tuning it, the string snapped and her eyes were terror-stricken as by the snapping of her universe.

She sang and she laughed: I love my brother.

I love my brother. I want crusades and martyrdom. I find the world too small.

Salted tears of defeat crystallized in the corners of her restless eyes.

But I never weep.

She picked up a mirror and looked at herself with love.

Narcisse gazing at himself in Lanvin mirrors. The Four Horsemen of the Apocalypse riding through the Bois. Tragedy rolling on cord tires.

The world is too small. I get tired of playing the guitar, of knitting, and walking, and bearing children. Men are small, and passions are short-lived. I get furious at stairways, furious at doors, at walls, furious at everyday life which interferes with the continuity of ecstasy.

But there is a martyrdom of tenseness, of fever, of living continuously like the firmament in full movement and in full effulgence.

You never saw the stars grow weary or dim. They never sleep.

She sat looking at herself in a hand mirror and searching for an eyelash which had fallen into her eye.

I married a man, Jeanne said, who had never seen painted eyes weep, and on the day of my wedding I wept. He looked at me and he saw a woman shedding enormous black tears, very black tears. It frightened him to see me shedding

black tears on my wedding night. When I heard
the bells ringing I thought they rang far too loud.
They deafened me. I felt I would begin to weep
blood, my ears hurt me so much. I coughed because the din was immense and terrifying, like the
time I stood next to the bells of Chartres. He said
the bells were not loud at all, but I heard them so
close to me that I could not hear his voice, and the
noise seemed like hammering against my flesh,
and I thought my ears would burst. Every cell in
my body began to burst, one by one, inside of
the immense din from which I could not escape.
I tried to run away from the bells. I shouted: stop
the bells from ringing! But I could not run away
from them because the sound was all round me
and inside me, like my heart pounding in huge
iron beats, like my arteries clamping like cym-
bals, like my head knocked against granite and
a hammer striking the vein on my temple. Ex-
plosions of sounds without respite which made
my cells burst, and the echoes of the cracking
and breaking in me rolled into echoes, struck me
again and again until my nerves were twisting and
curling inside me, and then snapped and tore at
the gong, until my flesh contracted and shrivelled
with pain, and the blood spilled out of my ears
and I could not bear any more . . . Could not bear

to attend my own wedding, could not bear to be married to man, because, because, because . . .

I LOVE MY BROTHER!

She shook her heavy Indian bracelets; she caressed her Orient blue bottles, and then she lay down again.

I am the most tired woman in the world. I am tired when I get up. Life requires an effort which I cannot make. Please give me that heavy book. I need to put something heavy like that on top of my head. I have to place my feet under the pillows always, so as to be able to stay on earth. Otherwise I feel myself going away, going away at a tremendous speed, on account of my lightness. I know that I am dead. As soon as I utter a phrase my sincerity dies, becomes a lie whose coldness chills me. Don't say anything, because I see that you understand me, and I am afraid of your understanding. I have such a fear of finding another like myself, and such a desire to find one! I am so utterly lonely, but I also have such a fear that my isolation be broken through, and I no longer be the head and ruler of my universe. I am in great terror of your understanding by which you penetrate into my world; and then I stand revealed and I have to share my kingdom with you.

But Jeanne, fear of madness, only the fear of
madness will drive us out of the precincts of our
solitude, out of the sacredness of our solitude.
The fear of madness will burn down the walls of
our secret house and send us out into the world
seeking warm contact. Worlds self-made and
self-nourished are so full of ghosts and monsters.

Knowing only fear, it is true, such a fear that
it chokes me, that I stand gasping and breathless,
like a person deprived of air; or at other times,
I cannot hear, I suddenly become deaf to the
world. I stamp my feet and hear nothing. I shout
and hear nothing of my shout. And then at times,
when I lie in bed, fear clutches me again, a great
terror of silence and of what will come out of this
silence towards me and knock on the walls of my
temples, a great mounting, choking fear. I knock
on the wall, on the floor, to drive the silence away.
I knock and I sing and I whistle persistently until I
drive the fear away.

When I sit before my mirror I laugh at myself.
I am brushing my hair. Here are a pair of eyes,
two long braids, two feet. I look at them like dice
in a box, wondering if I should shake them, would
they still come out and be ME. I cannot tell how
all these separate pieces can be ME. I do not exist.
I am not a body. When I shake hands I feel that

the person is so far away that he is in the other room, and that my hand is in the other room. When I blow my nose I have a fear that it might remain on the handkerchief.

Voice like a mistle thrush. The shadow of death running after each word so that they wither before she has finished uttering them.

When my brother sat in the sun and his face was shadowed on the back of the chair I kissed his shadow. I kissed his shadow and this kiss did not touch him, this kiss was lost in the air and melted with the shadow. Our love of each other is like one long shadow kissing, without hope of reality.

S HE LED ME INTO THE HOUSE OF INCEST.
It was the only house which was not in-
cluded in the twelve houses of the zodiac. It could
neither be reached by the route of the milky way,
nor by the glass ship through whose transparent
bottom one could follow the outline of the lost
continents, nor by following the arrows pointing
the direction of the wind, nor by following the
voice of the mountain echoes.

The rooms were chained together by steps—
no room was on a level with another—and all the
steps were deeply worn. There were windows
between the rooms, little spying-eyed windows,
so that one might talk in the dark from room to
room, without seeing the other's face. The rooms
were filled with the rhythmic heaving of the
sea coming from many sea-shells. The windows
gave out on a static sea, where immobile fishes
had been glued to painted backgrounds. Everything had been made to stand still in the house
of incest, because they all had such a fear of

movement and warmth, such a fear that all love and all life should flow out of reach and be lost!

Everything had been made to stand still, and everything was rotting away. The sun had been nailed in the roof of the sky and the moon beaten deep into its Oriental niche.

In the house of incest there was a room which could not be found, a room without window, the fortress of their love, a room without window where the mind and blood coalesced in a union without orgasm and rootless like those of fishes. The promiscuity of glances, of phrases, like sparks marrying in space. The collision between their resemblances, shedding the odor of tamarisk and sand, of rotted shells and dying seaweeds, their love like the ink of squids, a banquet of poisons.

Stumbling from room to room I came into the room of paintings, and there sat Lot with his hand upon his daughter's breast while the city burned behind them, cracking open and falling into the sea. There where he sat with his daughter the Oriental rug was red and stiff, but the turmoil which shook them showed through the rocks splitting around them, through the earth yawning beneath their feet, through the trees flaming up like torches, through the sky smoking and

smouldering red, all cracking with the joy and
terror of their love. Joy of the father's hand upon
the daughter's breast, the joy of the fear racking
through her. Her costume tightly pressed around
her so that her breasts heave and swell under
his fingers, while the city is rent by lightning,
and spits under the teeth of fire, great blocks of
a gaping ripped city sinking with the horror of
obscenity, and falling into the sea with the hiss of
the eternally damned. No cry of horror from Lot
and his daughter but from the city in flames, from
an unquenchable desire of father and daughter, of
brother and sister, mother and son.

I looked upon a clock to find the truth. The
hours were passing like ivory chess figures, striking piano notes, and the minutes raced on wires
mounted like tin soldiers. Hours like tall ebony
women with gongs between their legs, tolling
continuously so that I could not count them. I
heard the rolling of my heart-beats; I heard the
footsteps of my dreams, and the beat of time was
lost among them like the face of truth.

I came upon a forest of decapitated trees,
women carved out of bamboo, flesh slatted like
that of slaves in joyless slavery, faces cut in two by
the sculptor's knife, showing two sides forever
separate, eternally two-faced, and it was I who

had to shift about to behold the entire woman. Truncated unsymmetrical figures, eleven sides, eleven angles, in veined and vulnerable woods, fragments of bodies, bodies armless and headless. The torso of a tube-rose, the knee of Achilles, tubercles and excrescences, the foot of mummy in rotted wood, the veined docile wood carved into human contortions. The forest must weep and bend like the shoulders of men, dead figures inside of live trees. A forest animated now with intellectual faces, intellectual contortions. Trees become man and woman, two-faced, nostalgic for the shivering of leaves. Trees reclining, woods shining, and the forest trembling with rebellion so bitter I heard its wailing within its deep forest consciousness. Wailing the loss of its leaves and the failure of transmutation.

Further a forest of white plaster, white plaster eggs. Large white eggs on silver disks, an elegy to birth, each egg a promise, each half-shaped nascence of man or woman or animal not yet precise. Womb and seed and egg, the moist beginning being worshipped rather than its flowering. The eggs so white, so still, gave birth to hope without breaking, but the cut-down tree lying there produced a green live branch that laughed at the sculptor.

J EANNE OPENED ALL THE DOORS AND searched through all the rooms. In each room the startled guest blinked with surprise. She asked them: "Please hang up something out of your windows. Hang up a shawl, or a colored handker-chief, or a rug. I am going out into the garden. I want to see how many windows can be accounted for. I may thus find the room where my brother is hiding from me. I have lost my brother. I beg you, help me, every one of you." She pulled shawls off the tables, she took a red curtain down, a coral bedspread, a Chinese panel, and hung them out of the windows herself.

Then she rushed out into the garden of dead trees, over the lava paths, over the micha schist, and all the minerals on her path burned, the muscovite like a bride, the pyrite, the hydrous silica, the cinnabar, the azurite like a fragment of benefic Jupiter, the malachite, all crushed together, pressed together, melted jewels, melted planets, alchemized by air and sun and time and space, mixed into mineral fixity, the fixity of the fear of death and the fear of life.

Semen dried into the silence of rock and mineral. The words we did not shout, the tears unshed, the curse we swallowed, the phrase we shortened, the love we killed, turned into magnetic iron ore, into tourmaline, into pyrate agate, blood congealed into cinnabar, blood calcinated, leadened into galena, oxidized, aluminized, sulphated, calcinated, the mineral glow of dead meteors and exhausted suns in the forest of dead trees and dead desires.

Standing on a hill of orthoclase, with topaz and argentite stains on her hands, she looked up at the facade of the house of incest, the rusty ore facade of the house of incest, and there was one window with the blind shut tight and rusty, one window without light like a dead eye, choked by the hairy long arm of old ivy.

She trembled with the desire not to shriek, an effort so immense that she stood still, her blood unseen for the golden pallor of her face.

She struggled with her death coming: I do not love anyone; I love no one, not even my brother. I love nothing but this absence of pain, this cold neutral absence of pain.

Standing still for many years, between the moment she had lost her brother and the moment she had looked at the facade of the house of incest, moving in endless circles round the corners of the dreams, never reaching the end of her voyage, she apprehended all wonder through the rock-agedness of her pain, by dying.

And she found her brother asleep among the paintings.

Jeanne, I fell asleep among the paintings, where I could sit for many days worshipping your portrait. I fell in love with your portrait, Jeanne, because it will never change. I have such a fear of seeing you grow old, Jeanne; I fell in love with an unchanging you that will never be taken away from me. I was wishing you would die, so that no one could take you away from me, and I would love the painting of you as you would look eternally.

They bowed to one part of themselves only— their likeness.

Good night, my brother!

Good night, Jeanne!

With her walked distended shadows, stigmatized by fear. They carried their compact like a jewel on their breast; they wore it proudly like their coat of arms.

WALKED INTO MY OWN BOOK, SEEKING peace.

It was night, and I made a careless movement inside the dream; I turned too brusquely the corner and I bruised myself against my madness. It was this seeing too much, this seeing of a tragedy in the quiver of an eyelid, constructing a crime in the next room, the men and women who had loved before me on the same hotel bed.

I carry white sponges of knowledge on strings of nerves.

As I move within my book I am cut by pointed glass and broken bottles in which there is still the odor of sperm and perfume.

More pages added to the book but pages like a prisoner's walking back and forth over the space allotted him. What is it allotted me to say? Only the truth disguised in a fairytale, and this is the fairytale behind which all the truths are staring as behind grilled mosque windows. With veils. The moment I step into the cavern of my lies I drop into darkness, and see a mask which stares at me like the glance of a cross-eyed man; yet I am wrapped in lies which do not penetrate my soul, as if the lies I tell were like costumes.

LIES CREATE SOLITUDE

I walked out of my book into the paralytic's room.

He sat there among many objects under glass as in a museum. He had collected a box of paint which he never painted with, a thousand books with pages uncut, and they were covered with dust. His Spanish cape hung on the shoulders of a mannequin, his guitar lay with strings snapped like long disordered hair. He sat before a note book of blank pages, saying: I swallow my own words. I chew and chew everything until it deteriorates. Every thought or impulse I have is chewed into nothingness. I want to capture all my thoughts at once, but they run in all directions. If I could do this I would be capturing the nimblest of minds, like a shoal of minnows. I would reveal innocence and duplicity, generosity and calcula-tion, fear and cowardice and courage. I want to tell the whole truth, but I cannot tell the whole truth because I would have to write four pages at once, like four columns simultaneously, four pages to the present one, and so I do not write at all. I would have to write backwards, retrace my steps constantly to catch the echoes and the overtones.

His skin was transparent like that of a newborn child, and his eyes green like moss. He bowed to Sabina, to Jeanne, and to me: meet the modern Christ, who is crucified by his own nerves, for all our neurotic sins!

The modern Christ was wiping the perspiration which dripped over his face, as if he were sitting there in the agony of a secret torture. Paincarved features. Eyes too open, as if dilated by scenes of horror. Heavy-lidded, with a world-heavy fatigue. Sitting on his chair as if there were ghosts standing beside him. A smile like an insult. Lips edged and withered by the black scum of drugs. A body taut like wire.

In our writings we are brothers, I said. The speed of our vertigoes is the same. We arrived at the same place at the same moment, which is not so with other people's thoughts. The language of nerves which we both use makes us brothers in writing.

The modern Christ said: I was born without a skin. I dreamed once that I stood naked in a garden and that it was carefully and neatly peeled, like a fruit. Not an inch of skin left on my body. It was all gently pulled off, all of it, and then I was told to walk, to live, to run. I walked slowly at first, and the garden was very soft, and I felt the softness of the garden so acutely, not on the surface of my body, but all through it, the soft warm air and the perfumes penetrated me like needles through every open bleeding pore. All the pores open and breathing the softness, the warmth, and the smells. The whole body invaded, penetrated, responding, every tiny cell and pore active and breathing and trembling and enjoying. I shrieked with pain. I ran. And as I ran the wind lashed me, and then the voices of people like whips on me. Being touched! Do you know what it is to be touched by a human being!

He wiped his face with his handkerchief.

The paralytic sat still in the corner of the room.

You are fortunate, he said, you are fortunate to feel so much; I wish I could feel all that. You are at least alive to pain, whereas I . . .

Then he turned his face away, and just before he turned away I saw the veins on his forehead swelling, swelling with the effort he made, the inner effort which neither his tongue nor his body, nor his thoughts would obey.

If only we could all escape from this house of incest, where we only love ourselves in the other, if only I could save you all from yourselves, said the modern Christ.

But none of us could bear to pass through the tunnel which led from the house into the world on the other side of the walls, where there were leaves on the trees, where water ran beside the paths, where there was daylight and joy. We could not believe that the tunnel would open on day-light: we feared to be trapped into darkness again; we feared to return whence we had come, from darkness and night. The tunnel would narrow and taper down as we walked; it would close around us, and close tighter and tighter around us and stifle us. It would grow heavy and narrow and suffocate us as we walked.

Yet we knew that beyond the house of incest there was daylight, and none of us could walk towards it.

We all looked now at the dancer who stood at the center of the room dancing the dance of the woman without arms. She danced as if she were deaf and could not follow the rhythm of the music. She danced as if she could not hear the sound of her castanets. Her dancing was isolated and separated from music and from us and from the room and from life. The castanets sounded like the steps of a ghost.

She danced, laughing and sighing and breathing all for herself. She danced her fears, stopping in the center of every dance to listen to reproaches that we could not hear, or bowing to applause that we did not make. She was listening to a music we could not hear, moved by hallucinations we could not see.

My arms were taken away from me, she sang. I was punished for clinging. I clung. I clutched all those I loved; I clutched at the lovely moments of life; my hands closed upon every full hour. My arms were always tight and craving to embrace. I wanted to embrace and hold the light, the wind, the sun, the night, the whole world. I wanted to caress, to heal, to rock, to lull, to surround, to encompass. And I strained and I held so much that they broke; they broke away from me. Everything eluded me then. I was condemned not to hold.

Trembling and shaking she stood looking at her arms now stretched before her again.

She looked at her hands tightly closed and opened them slowly, opened them completely like Christ; she opened them in a gesture of abandon and giving; she relinquished and forgave, opening her arms and her hands, permitting all things to flow away and beyond her.

I could not bear the passing of things. All flowing, all passing, all movement choked me with anguish.

And she danced; she danced with the music and with the rhythm of earth's circles; she turned with the earth turning, like a disk, turning all faces to light and to darkness evenly, dancing towards daylight.